This Walker book belongs to:

_____

_____

_____

For Vanessa, my splendid collaborator – J.H.

For Mum – T.F.

First published 2006 by Walker Books Ltd
87 Vauxhall Walk, London SE11 5HJ
This edition published 2008
2 4 6 8 10 9 7 5 3 1
Text © 2006 Judy Hindley
Illustrations © 2006 Tor Freeman
The right of Judy Hindley and Tor Freeman to be identified as author and illustrator respectively of this work
has been asserted by them in accordance with the Copyright, Designs and Patents Act 1988
This book has been typeset in Lemonade
Printed in China
British Library Cataloguing in Publication Data:
a catalogue record for this book is available from the British Library
ISBN 978-1-4063-0516-6
www.walker.co.uk

Sleepy Places

Judy Hindley

illustrated by

Tor Freeman

WALKER BOOKS
AND SUBSIDIARIES
LONDON · BOSTON · SYDNEY · AUCKLAND

When you're yawning and nodding and flopping,
and ready to fall in a heap,
where do you choose for a nap or a snooze
– where is your favourite place to sleep?

A rabbit sleeps tight in its burrow;

a bird snuggles down in a tree.

A frog takes
a snooze in
the ooze of a pond;

SNORE

a rose makes
a bed for a bee.

Do you suppose you
could drowse in a rose,

or snooze in the ooze

like a frog?

A cat can nap on
somebody's hat;
a bear curls up
in a cave.

A fish may dream in
the reeds of a stream;

a seal lolls about
on a wave...

Can you imagine what dreams you'd have,

lolling about on a wave?

A swift can sleep
on the wing as it flies;

a horse
can sleep on
the hoof;

bats hang
upside
down from
their toes,
in rows
upon rows
in the roof.

If you were a bat,
you'd sleep like that,
upside down
in the roof!

A pup likes to sleep

in a quivering heap,

with a bundle of sisters and brothers.

Kangaroo joeys tuck themselves up in pockets attached to their mothers.

But what about you?

What place do you choose
– what sleepy place
for a nap
or a snooze?

A nest of
cushions,

a cave of quilts,

a bundle of pillows ...

a cot,

a pram?

A hammock,

a sofa,

a box,

a rug,

a comfy lap,

a cuddly arm?

Or would you choose your own little bed,
with your own little blanket and pillow,

and kisses and stories and teddies and things,
and somebody tucking you in?

Oh yes -
we each have a
favourite sleepy place...

Goodnight.

Goodnight.

Goodnight!